Amelia Ellicott's Garden

Dedication
For Julia. LS.
To: Cliff (AD), Jobi, Mr Lin, Lore, Susannah and Kathy. SMK.

First published in 2000 by Margaret Hamilton Books
PO Box 28, Hunters Hill NSW 2110 Australia
A Division of Scholastic Australia Pty Limited.
© text, Liliana Stafford, 2000. © illustrations, Stephen Michael King, 2000.
National Library of Australia Cataloguing-in-publication entry
Stafford, Liliana. Amelia Ellicott's garden.
ISBN 1 876289 33 3.
I. King. Stephen Michael. II. Title. A823.3

Stephen Michael King used ink and watercolour for the illustrations.

Typeset in Berkeley Medium.
Printed in Hong Kong.
10 9 8 7 6 5 4 3 2 1   0 1 2 3 4 5 / 0

Amelia Ellicott's Garden

Written by Liliana Stafford • Illustrated by Stephen Michael King

A Margaret Hamilton book from Scholastic Australia

long time ago, Amelia Ellicott's family owned most of Sampson Street, from the candy store on the corner to the traffic circle on the main road.

Now Amelia Ellicott and her cat Mustafah live at number fifty-six, next door to a three-story apartment complex, with a high fence in between.

Every day Amelia Ellicott works in her garden as if the apartments and the people who live in them don't exist. "This used to be such a nice neighborhood," she says to Mustafah.

Amelia Ellicott's garden is getting out of hand. The roses near the road are almost too big for her to prune, and her once-beautiful lawn is full of weeds. But she is proud of her home.

And she is immensely proud of her chickens.

Amelia Ellicott's chickens aren't just ordinary chickens. They are prize Pekin Bantams, the color of sunshine and marigolds.

Every morning Amelia Ellicott feeds them corn . . .

and every evening she visits
them and stays for a chat.

In the spring, she had waited anxiously for the new chicks to hatch. And, when the first tiny fluffball chicks poked out from under the wings of the brooding hens,

she wished,

just for a second,

that there was someone to show them to.

But there is no one, for Amelia Ellicott's family died a long time ago, and Mustafah refuses to be interested in chickens.

But Tony Timponi is interested. Every
evening before supper he sits on the
balcony of his third-story apartment
and watches the chickens scratching in
their yard.

Back home in Italy, Tony and his wife Donna kept chickens and goats and grew fruit trees and vegetables. Now they live in an apartment.

"Life is hard," says Tony Timponi, as he watches Amelia Ellicott's chickens. "Life is terribly hard."

Adrian Popa agrees. He looks down into Amelia Ellicott's garden and wishes he could have just the tiniest corner to grow cabbage and zucchini.

His neighbor Lin Li, sipping an early morning cup of cocoa, dreams of ducks paddling about on Amelia Ellicott's fish pond.

The Martinovitch children, trying to see over the fence, imagine a tire swing in the big mulberry tree.

And Nicolae Butau, hurrying to catch the bus, stops for
a moment to smell the roses.

But no one ever says a word. They are too shy. And besides,
Amelia Ellicott never even gives them the time of day.

Then one gray and wintery afternoon, there is a terrible storm,

and the wind whips around Sampson Street like a tornado.

Amelia Ellicott watches in horror as her garden flies past her: the red and white umbrella she bought for the patio, a pink rose bush, several potted plants, the garbage can, and the chicken house roof.

"No, not the chicken house!" yells Amelia Ellicott.

She runs outside just in time to see the wind fling the sheets of corrugated iron against the fence. Then it lifts them up and dumps them in the parking lot of the apartment complex.

Next come the chickens.

And finally Amelia Ellicott herself
with her skirt over the top of her head.

And in the pouring rain, all the neighbors run around chasing chickens or try to catch bits of Amelia Ellicott's garden.

Amelia Ellicott straightens her skirt. "Oh dear," she says. "What a mess."

"Not to worry," says Donna Timponi. "You come in and sit down. I'll make you a nice cup of tea."

While they drink tea in Donna Timponi's little kitchen, Tony Timponi and his neighbors catch all the chickens, even the rooster who is high up in the mulberry tree.

Then they carry all the sheets of corrugated iron into Amelia Ellicott's garden and nail them back on the chicken house roof.

Amelia Ellicott is so grateful she turns beet red. "Thank you," she says as politely as she can. "Thank you so much."

"We'll come tomorrow and help clean up," says Adrian Popa. "No fence for a while, eh?"

Amelia manages a smile. "No," she agrees, "no fence."

"You could grow cabbage in that patch," says Adrian thoughtfully.

"I like cabbage," says Amelia, "and zucchini. We used to grow zucchini over there. Do you think . . . ?"

The following spring Amelia Ellicott's chickens hatch

twelve tiny fluffball chicks,

and Amelia shows them off to everyone.